To: Harper & Pax,

Read On!!

[signature]

BILLY

THE DENTIST

William "Billy" Zenga grew up in Fort Lauderdale Florida. Billy received his undergraduate degree from Florida State University, graduating Summa Cum Laude with a Major in Biochemistry in 2012. After Florida State, Billy attended Nova Southeastern University in Davie Florida for dental school where he graduated in 2016.

Billy attended the VA hospital in West Palm Beach, Florida for his residency before deciding to follow in his father's footsteps and take over the family practice. When not working on teeth, Billy enjoys playing ice hockey, golf, softball, and spending time with his friends and family.

BILLY'S FAMILY

BILLY'S DAD

Joe Garrick is the author of "Billy the Dentist" as well as "Whose Hoof Is That?". Joe is a North Carolina native who grew up in Hickory, NC and attended "The" Appalachian State University. Joe currently works in sales for a data analytics company in the healthcare industry. Joe is also an aspiring custom hat maker and the occasional wedding officiant.

Joe has always had a love for music, especially for rap and hip hop (and he even has a little musical talent himself). Although Joe's hip hop career hasn't quite taken off yet, he thought it would be nice to transition those creative skills into a different avenue that will hopefully reach a lot of people. Joe loves to make others laugh and the goal of all of his books so far is to do just that.

Check out Joe's other book "Whose Hoof Is That?"

at www.whosehoofisthat.com

Some people are born with wisdom teeth,
Most of us grow k-9's and molars.

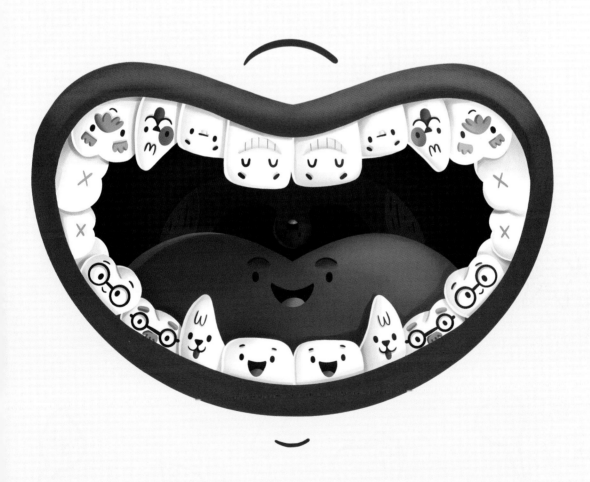

We all go to the dentist,

Some of us go in strollers.

From the start, you will learn

It's important to keep your teeth clean.

That's why you must always brush
And floss in between!

Popcorn has kernels
And sugar is sweet.

Be careful when you eat them

As they can really damage your teeth!

Your first set of teeth you will lose
And some teeth will be found.

At night if you put them under your pillow

The Tooth Fairy may visit,

Without ever making a sound.

Your grown-up teeth will come in
And may look a bit silly.

But you should never worry

Because here to help you...

Is your dentist named Billy!

Billy will make your teeth feel good

And help to fix your smile.

So you can feel proud

And show your whole family

The best smile they've seen in a while!

So remember going to the dentist is great!
You will have a very clean mouth
When you leave.

Now while you wait for your appointment

You will have a copy of this book to read.

Billy

Joe

Billy met Joe in 2020 when his sister

Lindsay and Joe's good friend Alex got married.

The idea for "Billy the Dentist" came about during

the wedding weekend festivities in Islamorada, FL.

Billy and Joe immediately became friends and

the book came to life in February of 2021.